I'M Alex!
I'M Two!

Story and Illustrations By

Joyce Ann Landon

To order additional copies of this book, contact:
Xlibris
844-714-8691
www.Xlibris.com
Orders@Xlibris.com

ISBN: Softcover   978-1-4568-0683-5
         EBook   978-1-6641-8233-2

Print information available on the last page

Rev. date: 06/25/2021

Hi! I'm Alex! Do you see my two fingers? I am two years old today! I want to invite you to my birthday party! Guess who came to my birthday party? Why, it is....

SPIDERMAN! Spiderman shows my older brother, Jacob, and me how to make web fingers! We are trying to follow his directions! Do our fingers look just like Spiderman's web fingers?

Now Spiderman shows my older brother, Jacob, and me how to make BIG MUSCLES! See how we are doing! We are trying to follow his directions! Don't our muscles look BIG? Wow! This is great!

Spiderman shows me how to fly! I really like flying!! I wonder if I can fly as well as Spiderman can. This really feels good!! My big brother, Jacob, loves watching me!

Spiderman gave me a Spiderman ball to throw in
that white net you see! I threw the Spiderman ball
and got it right into the white net while I kept looking
at Spiderman! He's so cool! He's so big and he can
do so many things! I want to be like him!

Spiderman also gave me this BIG, BOUNCY Spiderman ball to play with! That was so nice of him to give me another ball to play with! I just love to play with this ball! I like to make this big ball BOUNCE, BOUNCE, BOUNCE!!

At my birthday party I got a hockey stick as a gift!
Spiderman gave me a special Spiderman ball! Here
I am hitting the Spiderman ball with my brand new
hockey stick!

I love to build things! Here I am at the Hands on Museum with a tool box! You have to match the tools and find exactly where they belong! I love holding these tools and pretending I'm making something important! I AM A   BUILDER!!

I am still at the Hands on Museum! I told you how I like to build things! Well, here I am trying to build a real high wall with big foam blocks and big boxes that I found at the Hands on Museum! Wait until you see what I do with them!

You probably guessed right! I threw myself on all the big foam blocks and the big boxes and I knocked them right down!! That was FUN! Whee-e!

Here I am on our back patio! These cups once had plants in them! Mommy planted them. I took this empty carton and turned it upside down on my lap. Then I put my finger on top of each cup and listened to the sound it made. It went "POP"! I played with this made up toy for a long, long time!

Now I am at my favorite outside park! I am going down the blue slide really, really, fast! This is lots and lots of fun!

I go to the bouncy, bouncy place and I love to go down an "inflatable" slide! This is the very first slide I learned to go down! I kept going down on this slide over and over and over again!

One of the places I love to go to is the library in the city where I live! I am listening to the storyteller! I am sitting on the letter "D"! The story is about a rocket! I love rockets!! After storytime I made a rocket at craft time!

Another thing I like to do at the library is sit on a chair and use the computer! I love to sit on the chair and make the keys go with my fingers! I really like to watch the moving objects on the computer screen! I can sit here a long time!

The next thing I do at the library is go to the back of the room where the train sets are! I love the train sets! When I was a little baby I would crawl up on top of the train set! I wasn't allowed to stay there. The library people didn't like it when I did this.

Now I STAND by the train set and push the train cars along! Because I am a builder, I know how to hook the train cars together! I am two years old and I know a lot!

At the back of the library there is a table with lots of puzzles! I like to put things together and I really, really like putting puzzles together. Here I am working on a "shapes" puzzle! I just put the red circle where it should go in the puzzle. I know how to say the word, "circle"!

There are also crayons on the table at the back of the library! I love to take the big crayons and color on paper! Here I am using the big red crayon! Do you see what I just colored with my red crayon? This is fun!

After library, I like to go to the place where you can
go on machines! Here I am sitting on my knees so
that I can reach the steering wheel! Now I make the
steering wheel turn! I like to figure out how things
work! I am a builder and I also like to fix things!

But, at the end of the day the place I like to be best is at home with my family! Here I am playing with my big brother, Jacob! I love my big brother and I love my mommy and daddy!

Printed in the United States
by Baker & Taylor Publisher Services